Trapped in the Game

Tamicka Higgins

© 2017

Disclaimer

This is a work of fiction. Names, places, characters and events are all fictitious for the reader's pleasure. Any similarities to real people, places, events, living or dead are all coincidental.

This book contains sexually explicit content that is intended for ADULTS ONLY (+18).

The "Last" One

"I know you ain't lightin' a blunt in my fuckin' car right now."

"Man! We 'bout to be paid! You can buy a new one. I needa zone."

"You *needa* put that shit out before you bitch-slapped."

"Come on, Black! Relax a little bit. Here, take a hit."

I took it. Fuck, I probably needed it. We'd been staking out that pharmacy for all of two weeks. Buzzy got word from his man inside that they were getting ready to relocate. That meant no cash pick-ups and no inventory and the security team was cut. The only thing we had to do was get in without triggering any alarms.

The problem was that his man inside insisted on being there for the heist. He played it off like he didn't trust us, but that fuckin' junkie just wanted first dibs on the pills and syringes. I used to have a policy—never work with junkies. I waived too much of my better judgement hoping that this would be my final job.

"Where the fuck is your boy at anyway? He supposed to be here at one."

"He'll be here, man. You know how Lenny is."

"No, I don't. That's the problem. All I know is what I've heard of 'em, and it ain't good. He better not show up high."

"Man, *we* high. Don't be so judgmental."

I couldn't be too sure. Buzzy had just tried kicking the hard shit himself. I didn't like how excited he was—especially then. It was an early sign of some dumb nigga shit getting ready to take place. I played along despite the red flags. Technically, it was *his* connect. I was sure to bring an extra glock, just in case niggas got silly. There are few better motivators than a loaded gun to your head.

"Look, there they go."

They drove up in a black Suburban blasting the bass. Typical wide-eyed amateur shit. I told them to stay unseen and even less heard. Fuck it though; I didn't have time to preach proper burglary etiquette. I was just happy they showed up. Lenny had the keys and codes to get in. I knew I'd have to play along with these assholes if I wanted everything to run smoothly. As always, I was ready to jump if they didn't. You can call it paranoia if you want. I've been around the block enough times to identify incompetence.

"Put that out. Let's go."

They signaled us to run around back and pull up behind the doors where the trucks are unloaded. Businesses are always more concerned with *looking* more secure than they are. When we got to the door, they were already fidgeting with the locks.

"What's good, y'all?"

"Buzzy! What's happenin', partna!"

"Lenny, you stupid motherfucker! Shut the hell up!"

I didn't recognize the guy that was yelling at Lenny. Bald guy, about six-five and the width of a building. I'd expected him to bring some muscle; even a junkie knows not to trust the motherfuckas that come in a different car.

I didn't plan on pullin' any sideways shit. Even if I had, the nigga he had with him looked like he had killed a few people in his day. A smart man would second-guess trying to get the upper-hand.

"Hey, Brotha, I'm Vic."

"Black. The nigga with the stupid grin is Buzzy."

"I know Buzzy. Little nigga that used to smoke dust and show his dick to prostitutes."

There's nothing like a good laugh to ease the tension. Besides, Buzzy's happy ass needed his mood knocked down a few pegs.

"Why you gotta bring that up, motherfucker? That was like two years ago."

"It happened, ain't it?"

As much as I enjoyed seeing Buzzy squirm, we had a narrow window of time before the cameras were turned back on.

"We can bitch later. We gotta get this lock off."

"I got it."

Vic twisted the lock and broke it off the pulley chain. I liked this guy already. I didn't have to worry too much about keepin' the knuckleheads under control after that. Two adults could get this job done and get the money, while the junkies ogled over the mountains of free high.

Lenny ducked and rolled under the security gate. It took him a few tries but he was able to shut off the alarm. I couldn't believe that the shit was working. We sent Buzzy in first to make sure the coast was clear. I figured—worst case scenario—if there's any security they'd be wise enough to just send the junkie on his way. Best case, they'd bring his ass to county for a few nights so he could dry out.

Don't get me wrong. Buzzy's my boy, but that nigga needed some saving that he wasn't gonna get on the streets. Rehabs weren't necessarily an option for him anymore. To this day a piece of me wishes that it was him they caught that day.

It seemed like the coast was clear. We left Lenny outside to stand guard. We didn't really need him to—the alarm was shut off—but I think we all just silently agreed that it was best to keep him away from the pills. Every team's got a wild-card. You'd do well to remember to keep them out of the deck.

He pulled the car up to the gate and shut the lights off. Buzzy blessed him with the clip of the blunt from the car to keep him occupied.

Getting into the place was child's play after that. Though it was still too early to breathe a sigh of relief.

***

We'd just finished cleaning out the pharmacy. We had Buzzy hold on to the duffel bags while we tried to crack open the safe. Vic took a drill to the lock. We'd almost gotten out of there. Just fifteen more fuckin' minutes and we all could have gone home that night and then gone our separate ways.

The car horn blasted loud enough for us to hear it from deep inside the place. We'd agreed that'd be the signal that it was time to get the hell outta there. The problem was, that it was supposed to be three quick bursts then stop. The air horn sounded and just kept going. We freaked the fuck out, jumped over the counter, and ran back to the receiving doors where we'd come in. Lenny had fallen asleep on the wheel, blunt in hand.

Buzzy and I ran to our car to load up the bags. Vic went over to the driver's side of the car and slapped Lenny awake. I didn't have time for that shit. I took my mask off and got in the car. I waited for them to sort it out while Buzzy tried to close the receiving gate.

"What the fuck, Vic?"

"Have you lost your motherfuckin' mind, negro?"

"What happened?"

"Get your junkie ass out of the car!"

We let them bicker. Who could really give a fuck in the moment? We didn't get the money, but we had four duffel bags filled with top-of-the-line narcs. Percs, Zany's, Adderall, Codeine. We could keep all of Hollywood high for the next couple of years with this one pull. Street value, that's a block worth of mansions along with a few new cars in each driveway. I celebrated in low laughter while we waited for Vic and Lenny to finish their lover's quarrel. We probably should have stopped them. They just kept getting louder.

"Why I got to get out the car? You get in the passenger seat!"

"Lenny, I swear to God I will kill you and leave your body here!"

"Do it, you Ving Rhames lookin' motherfucka!"

I was about to get out of the car to put an end to the nonsense. I guess Vic wasn't as on top of his shit as I thought. Lenny had a fucking power trip over car keys. That's kid shit. About thirty seconds after that we heard the sirens. Vic finally agreed to get in the backseat. Police sirens will give a nigga a hefty dose of *act-right* real fuckin' quick.

Pressure

Lenny started the car and, just as Vic grabbed the door handle, two beat cops pulled into the back alleyway. Lenny put the car in drive and sped past them. It was a fuckin' selfish move. To make matters worse, it tipped them off that this was more than just an average dispute.

Vic was stuck out on the street, with the receiving doors wide open, and the lock to the gate broken off just a few feet away from him. Buzzy and I melted into our seats and watched the whole thing go down from side-view mirrors.

One of the cops went to the car and called back-up to chase Lenny down, "Dispatch we've got a 10-80 heading north off Grant Street. One suspect detained."

Lenny did a good job of knocking around on the curb as he made his getaway. His car would be easy to find with all the dents in the fuckin' hood. I'll say it again—never work with a junkie.

Vic complied. Smart dude. Officers around there had itchy trigger fingers for threatening-looking black people. They'd just killed Buzzy's brother a few months earlier for selling loose cigarettes by the local bodega. He was about half of Vic's size and they still unloaded half a clip into him. They would've had no problem puttin' a few extra rounds in Vic's head if he acted any kind of suspicious.

They put cuffs on Vic, threw him in the car, and waited for their back-up. They taped up the area. When they started skulking around the back lot, we started to get anxious. The important thing was to stay silent and steady.

Buzzy and I had four duffel bags full of stolen merchandise and only a few minutes before the street would be swarming with the cops. We watched, ready for a shootout while they investigated the crime scene.

"Yo Black," he whispered. "What the fuck we gon' do, man?"

"Shut the fuck up. I'm thinkin'."

I'd garnered a reputation for having the gift of gab. I guess it helped keep me outta jail that long. But, with the cops on their way and us stuck around the corner from the scene of the crime, there wasn't much sweet-talking that could get us out of here without them at least searching the vehicle.

I had nothing.

"Yo, Black, come on, man, we gotta go."

I could hardly think straight between Buzzy's incessant ranting and raving.

"I can't go to jail, man. I can't go back. There's motherfuckas lookin' for me in there. I don't want to die, Black!"

He pulled a flask from his pocket and took a swig. "What am I gonna tell my momma? She sick, Black. I think she got colitis! My momma gon' be shittin' the bed, Black! Who gon' clean up my momma!"

"Buzzy, shut the fuck up! And take that damn mask off."

"These my last words. Hail Mary, full of grace… I don't know the rest of the words, Black. Aw, shit! We going to hell!"

He was losing his fuckin' mind. I've been tellin' him to stay off that shit for years. There's something about addicts; you don't even realize how bad off they are until shit goes south. I figured that I could use it to my advantage if we got caught. I still had to figure out a fuckin' excuse for us being on a dead-end street that late.

More cop cars started showing up. We were low under the dashboard—we were lucky they drove right past us. They set up some roadblocks down both ends of the street. We'd have to go through them to get back to the main road. If we could make it there, we'd be free. I thought of something crazy that might work. It was risky, but it was that or be discovered hiding. I figured we were fucked no matter what. I may as well go out with some effort.

As Buzzy hyperventilated and finished off his drink, I sat up in my seat, put the key in the ignition and turned on the car.

"Black? What you doing, Black?"

I turned on the headlights and started to turn the wheel. "Get up, Buzzy. Sit right. Put your flask away."

He got up and I slowly pulled away from the curb as the police cars parked behind us. I had to be going about five miles an hour, but we were moving.

"Black! I don't want to go to jail, Black!"

I rolled our windows down and lit a cigarette. "Take one." I gave one to Buzzy to calm his nerves. It wasn't laced with anything, but I knew that if he was busy smoking he would be too occupied to run his fuckin' mouth.

We pulled up to the checkpoint. The four officers had just gotten there. They were all leaning on their cars, drinking coffee. They seemed like they were barely awake; that meant they'd be easy to charm. No one wants a part in needless violence, not even the boys in blue.

We were flagged down between a line of freshly set-up traffic cones. One officer approached the car with his flashlight in one hand, and the other on his state-issued glock.

Buzzy took such a hard pull from his cigarette that you could smell the filter burning. I don't think he knew. I don't even think he really gave a fuck. "You better not piss yourself in my car, Buzzy." I told him in a calm voice, while the officer came up to the window.

"Fuck you, Black."

I put my license and registration on the dashboard, flicked my cigarette, put my hands on the wheel and took a deep breath.

"How you doing today, son?"

"Good, officer, and you?"

"Fine, fine. License and registra—Oh, there it is. Get pulled over often?" he joked.

"Don't you see my face? It ain't a normal day if it don't happen twice."

"A sense of humor, finally." He handed my paperwork back to me and leaned his head into the window. "You know, I tell ya; this is such a stressful job most days. They call us up at random and don't even tell us what for."

It was a smooth tactic, but I knew the game. He wanted to stress us—see if we would break. I just prayed that Buzzy would be able to keep his shit together for just a few more minutes. I let the officer keep talking our ears off while I smiled and nodded.

"Is your friend okay? Looks like he's seen a ghost."

"No. But he'll be okay. A little too much fun tonight."

"Oh. I've been there. Well, you boys have a good night. And try to stay off of the expressway. Some lunatic is out there leading us on a merry little chase. They always end up on that damn thing."

"You too, officer."

He tapped the top of the car twice and waved us through. Buzzy took an exhale. We passed the checkpoint and turned onto the main road, being sure to avoid the ramp leading to the expressway. We drove in silence for a minute, until I had to ask, "So, your Momma's got colitis for real?"

Buzzy lit a blunt and looked at me with the *fuck you* face. "My momma's got a lot of shit."

We laughed and made our way to the safe house as a slew of other cop cars sped past us. They must've figured. Who gave a fuck though? We got away.

We did it.

Bulk

Buzzy came through. We got to the safe house a little after three, unloaded the duffel bags from the trunk and crept back in as quietly as we could. Once we knew that we were in the clear, Buzzy immediately wanted to party to relieve the tension. He tried calling over some thots that he'd been trying to fuck for who knows how long.

While he laid out on the couch and made his phone calls, I moved the bags to my bedroom and took inventory. We had everything: pills, lean, syringes, opiates, steroids, you name it. We had enough to take care of you and everybody that you know. As reckless as Buzzy was, fiends tend to be really good at math. I called him in to give his *professional* estimate.

The corporations were selling some of the shit for eighty to one hundred dollars a pill. Street value—depending on how we sold it—meant that we'd have a little over five million dollars to split two ways. It was fucked up to cut Lenny and Vic out, but those niggas knew the score before they jumped in. If you ain't there for the count, you forfeit your amount. That was a key rule to this shit. Always has been.

Buzzy's hoes showed up about twenty minutes later. I'd heard him arguing with them, but it sounded like they changed their tune once they found out that Buzzy could get them on "the hottest shit since Satan". I didn't have the energy to get annoyed. Frankly, I was just as fuckin' excited as he was.

This was the Big Hit; the final play. After a life of gang-banging and slinging mid-level shit, I could finally take my piece and leave the lifestyle for good. All we'd have to do is find some dealers willing to buy in bulk. Fuck it, I didn't mind taking a little bit of a loss. When this day started, I was worried about a bunch of normal shit. Four hours later, I was a millionaire. Thank God for small miracles.

I'm uptight sometimes. That's just because the game requires it. From that night on, there should've been no reason to stress about anything ever again. Why not let loose a little? I stashed the shit under the floorboard in my bedroom and locked it. When I got into the living room, Buzzy had already had a few joints lit sitting between two of the most "hood-pretty" bitches that money could buy. I popped open some liquor and joined them on the couch with a bottle of painkillers. I deserved to feel every moment of that night. It was supposed to be the beginning of the rest of my life.

Me and Buzzy fucked the shit out of those girls that night. No hang-ups, no comedowns, and no drama. We were new millionaires—already living like kings.

***

I don't think we woke up until like one in the afternoon. I was back in my bedroom with one of the prostitutes. Apparently we'd gotten a little wild. The whole place looked like a damn frat-house.

When I got up to get some water, Buzzy was ass naked on the couch with the other one. I basked in the serenity for a second. I knew that once he came to, it would be back to business until we got all this shit divided and settled.

I poured myself a bowl of cereal and turned on the news. I'll admit that I was curious to see if we had made their line-up of popular reports.

"One in custody and another at large as the investigation into the burglary at pharmaceutical giant Gold's Pharmacy wages on. The two suspects are believed to have broken into the warehouse early last night—stealing an estimated five million

dollars' worth of prescription medication among a variety of other paraphernalia."

"What the fuck you watching, Black?"

"Shut it for a minute, Buzzy."

I turned the volume up.

"Officers have stated that the suspect at large led them on a chase through the city streets and into the woods—where he was last seen. The suspect has been identified as Leonard McDowell. We are told that McDowell is to be considered armed and extremely dangerous. We are warning that if you happen to encounter McDowell, do not approach. Please call your local authorities with any and all information."

"Oh shit, Black. That nigga on the run!"

It was a humbling thing to know. Not only did we not have to share any of the profit, but now we wouldn't even have to worry too much about gettin' snitched on. Cops won't offer a deal to someone that gives them that hard of a time.

It did put us in a bit of a situation though. Now that the shit was national news, we couldn't be caught around here trying to peddle any of *our* shit. Even if a motherfucka was dumb enough to buy it off of us, the paper trail would lead right back to the neighborhood. Buzzy and I both had priors—we'd make the shortlist for sure.

It'd crossed my mind that Lenny may be a problem to a lesser extent. He didn't know where the safe house was, but he knew Buzzy well enough to throw him under the bus. Nothing would stick without evidence though. The point was, we had to move all that shit as quickly as possible. No drugs, no case.

"Shit!"

"What's up, Black?"

"Get these bitches out of here, Buzzy."

"You sure, man? I was gon' get me a little morning dome."

"Now!"

"You got it!"

Buzzy put on his boxers, knocked the one chick off of the couch and then dragged the other from out of my bedroom, while I poured myself a drink.

"Bitches! Vamanos! Chop-Chop!"

I blessed them each with a few hundred for their *services*—I'm pretty sure they stole some of our weed—but we could just call it even. We had bigger issues to worry about.

"You still cool with Carlos, down over on East?"

"You mean the nigga with the lazy-eye. Hell yeah. Where you think this weed came from? *Es mi hermano.*"

"Stop acting Spanish."

"Hey man, I'm one-sixteenth Ecuadorian on my baby-momma's side. So what you need him for?"

The plan was simple. Carlos was an illegal from over in Mexico. He had a temper, but word got out that he also had a sweet spot for his people across the border. He'd make his money out here and always bring it back home. If there was anyone we knew that could dilute the circle of distribution, it'd be him. We'd take a hit, but it'd be well worth it to get this shit outta here.

"We shoulda got the fuckin' money first."

"We'll be aight, Black. I'mma call him now."

My mind had already drifted to the next problem. How the fuck do we keep Lenny from talking? It's never good to overthink, but it's always good to think ahead. I'd have to go see him at some point, but first thing's first.

***

We packed up a bag with a sample of each drug, along with a little cocaine to sweeten the deal. Buzzy always kept a brick or two at the house. He used to say that it was his "retirement fund". I knew he was taking bumps every now and again, but his nose wasn't priority at the moment, and his stash may have proven to be the ultimate social lubricant for the negotiation.

"What you mean bring 'em both? Nigga, you done lost your damn mind."

"So then what's *your* plan?" I asked him.

"We just bring him the fucking samples and if he buys it, he buys it."

"Then what?"

We argued about it for a little while before we left. When I kindly reminded that he was already rich, it seemed like a lightbulb went off in his head and shut down his stupid.

"Aight. But if he wants to do some lines, I'm doing 'em too."

"Do I look like I give a fuck? Just get the job done!"

We got in the car with a suitcase full of product and drove over to the East Side where we knew Carlos was likely to be outside—already drunk—sipping on a Corona talking shit about the country that he snuck into. It was the best time to make a deal with him without shit getting violent.

Loco

Carlos and I had a history of not getting along too well. A few of my guys took out a few of his, and vice versa. We'd come to the mutual understanding to stay off of each other's turf and out of the way. The last time we'd met was after a pretty thorough gun fight some months back. We both got paid, but there was still some bad blood between us.

Lucky enough, he didn't count any of that drama against Buzzy, who'd proven to be one of his favorite customers. Had it been anybody else, they would have ended up buried in the woods somewhere, but Buzzy was well-respected enough to get away with it. It helped to keep the channels of trade open between the races.

It was known that we didn't get along but, at the end of the day, business is business. He and I didn't often agree on much—but we agreed on money. Anything that would help with the "come-up" he was game for; I just had to play it right.

I let Buzzy drive to make sure we gave off the appearance that he was the one pulling the strings. If they knew it was me, they might've acted funny. I held my gun on the side just in case one of his goons got antsy.

When we pulled up, Carlos was right where we thought he'd be—outside his house on the stoop drinking a forty-ounce and smoking a blunt.

"You see, man. That ain't no Corona."

"Are you kidding me right now?"

"I'm just saying, that was racist."

"It wasn't racist. It was an observation."

"Man, whatever. You coming in?"

"Nah. Go handle it. Just don't come back with *nothing*."

"Don't even trip, Black. I told you, Carlos *es mi hermano*."

"Would you hurry the fuck up before I change my mind?"

"Yeah, yeah. I'll call you when it's time to talk numbers."

I wasn't really anxious about Buzzy fucking up fresh out the gate. I made sure that he was going in relatively sober so that he wouldn't pull any junkie shit. I was more worried about how bad he'd be on the way out. Carlos liked to party and Buzzy liked to compete. I pushed the thought down. Worst case scenario, he'd come back a little hyper. Shit, the coke might make the whole thing go by a lot quicker.

He jogged across the street over to Carlos's looking suspect as fuck. The two welcomed each other in one of the loudest fucking exchanges of Spanglish that I'd ever heard. But, they were laughing so it couldn't have been all bad. I waited for a few minutes after the two of them went inside to make sure that everything had been cordial.

Once I was sure that Buzzy was safe, I got out of the car, leaned on the hood and lit a cigarette. I needed the peace. The last twelve hours had given me plenty of shit to think about.

Carlos left some of his guys outside to keep an eye on me. They did their usual—throwing up gang signs and mean muggin'. I ignored them and kept one hand on my gun.

Enemy territory can be a bitch when you invite yourself.

***

I set the alarm on my phone for an hour and fifteen minutes. I knew that Buzzy liked to bullshit in stressful situations. A little over an hour should've been enough time for him to make the deal, snort some *get-well* and get the hell out.

Despite us having everything pretty much in check, I couldn't shake that calm before the storm feeling that I get in my gut whenever bullshit is about to be introduced into my life. I never really trusted the quiet—a nasty side-effect of my line of work.

I lit another cigarette and watched the kids play on the street. It was fun to see innocence like that again. I'd been mostly blind to good things since my son died, but I spectate with little issue at that point. I don't know what it was about that day. I guess it was because I thought that I'd be done with this life soon. Finally free to start on my new beginning. It was the kind of feeling they make songs about. For a split second, I was able to forget who I was and what I'd done. For a second, I was *me* again; who I was *before* the bullshit. It was a fleeting moment of ignorant bliss.

And that's all it was. Just as quickly as the kids had congregated, they'd started to fight. There were no other adults around except for Carlos's expendable team of assholes. They loved to watch a good dogfight. I knew they wouldn't stop them, so the responsibility would have to fall on me. It was either that or watch a kid get beat half to death. The last thing that I needed was for a good Samaritan to call the police. I thought *fuck it*, I could use the good karma.

I let them scrap about for a few minutes though, until I was bored. I'll admit that it was entertaining to watch them whale on each other. Ass-whoopings also tend to provide some unique life experience. You'll never know where you stand on the hierarchy if you ain't tested. When one of them picked up a brick I took my cue to play ref.

"Hey, you little motherfuckas! Break it up!"

The biggest kid always feels the need to talk back. "Or what?"

"Before I come over there and beat you like your daddy shoulda'!"

Of course, he sized me up and tightened his grip on the brick in his hand. I responded politely by flashing him my loaded semi. I think he damn near pissed himself. He scattered along with all the other runts except for the one that was bleeding on the ground.

He was surprisingly calm after getting what had to be the beating of his life. I checked my phone. I still had about an hour before the alarm would go off and there was no sign of Buzzy anyhow. Carlos's guys had been at attention. I may have overplayed my hand by intervening, so I took the opportunity to get away from them.

I went over to the kid and helped him up. It was a bad idea, but I sympathized. That first public beat down could fuck a kid up if no one's there to coach him through it. I just kept thinking about the karma, so I took on the role of *hood-guru* against my better judgement.

"That's a hell of a beating you just took."

"I'm fine."

"The gash on your head says different. What the hell were you fighting for anyway?"

"I was tryna get my chain back."

"Ah. So they got you for your pride?"

"No. They just got the pendant. The link is broken though."

The chain was big for a kid. It had to have been given to him by an older guy in his family. I'll hand it to him that it was nice. But the good ones don't break that easy. I figured I'd tell him, if I ever saw him again. He'd been beat down enough that day. "Well, I'll tell you what, little man... What's your name?"

"Darius."

"Aight. Listen, Darius, one of two things has to happen right now."

"Uh-huh."

"Either you got to go to the hospital and get stitched up—"

"I'm not going to the doctor."

"Okay, okay. Relax. Or, I gotta make sure that you get home okay."

"Why?"

"Let's just say that I could use the walk."

We went about three blocks over from Carlos's. We got to talking a little bit. Darius was twelve. He and his parents had moved out here a few years back. He hadn't seen his father in a few weeks. Shit like that is common around here. He didn't seem too tore up over it.

There was no need to question that any further, so I didn't. His mom sounded good enough though. Another hood stereotype. Young chick had a baby by a gangster. I was happy to hear that she was a nurse. She worked nights, so it meant she would be home. It was a relief for me. I thought that I could just drop the little nigga off and be back on my way—good karma accomplished.

"You sure your mother's home?"

"She was when I left."

"You think she'll be able to take care of this knot behind your head?"

"Yeah. She used to do it for my dad all the time."

"Good. I'mma need you to stop getting your ass beat, by the way."

"I don't fight a lot."

We stopped just in front of the house. I don't waste my time with preaching to people, but you've got to teach lessons to kids whenever you get a chance to. Worst thing it'll do is send them off in the right direction.

"And you don't always *have* to fight. Your mind can hit harder than any fist *if* you know how to use it."

"What if they want to fight me?"

It was a good question. One that I didn't think that I had the answer for. Turns out I did.

"Take up boxing."

I knocked on his door and waited for his mother to answer. His head was bleeding pretty bad. I'm actually still shocked that he was able to keep on his toes. The conversation probably helped keep him from blacking out.

I couldn't help but be a little pissed off. Sure, kids fight and all that, but the way he got his ass beat was unacceptable. Not his fault. I blamed the parents. I checked my phone and saw that I had a half-hour left. Didn't think it would hurt to set his mom straight too, even if it was just to keep the kid alive an extra day.

Price

"Oh my God, Darius!"

His mother came to the door and looked at me like I was the fucking grim reaper. I cut her off before she aimed her anger at me.

"Hold on. Let me explain."

I knew that she would go crazy at the sight of her son bleeding from his head—what parent wouldn't?—but I didn't expect her to have a full-on breakdown. I calmed her down and told her to breathe.

"Listen, you're a nurse, right?"

"Yeah..." she said, inspecting the back of her son's head. She sent him to the bathroom and invited me in to sit on the couch while she grabbed her first-aid kit and tended to his wound. The house looked barely lived in. Like they'd either been on their way out or were recently robbed. I sat down and looked around while she ran back and forth looking for towels and peroxide.

While she patched him up, Darius and I took turns telling her what happened. I was impressed. Most women I know freeze in situations like that. Once she'd been able to calm down she was surprisingly on top of shit.

Darius was cleaned up in a matter of minutes. She sent him to his room to play video games and warned him not to go to sleep. When she finished cleaning up the blood and tissues, she thanked me from the kitchen and offered me a drink. I had twenty minutes to spare. Why not get tight before heading back?

"Do you have whiskey?"

"...Uh... Yeah. You know the sun's still out, right?"

I was used to critical tones, but her familiarity was annoying.

"You tryna say something?"

"No, not at all. Do you want ice?"

She got over herself quickly and actually poured herself a glass too then joined me in the living room. She was wearing a tank-top and basketball shorts. I did my best not to stare at her hard nipples. But damn, the Lord really took his time with this one. She looked like she was fresh out of bed and still could've posed for *Vanity Fair*.

"I'm sorry. What did you say that your name was again?"

"Black."

"Black? Like the color?"

"It's actually a shade. But, yeah. Somethin' like that."

"Okay, Mr. Black. Well, I'm Layla. Layla Price. Thank you very much for helping my son. He's been having a rough time lately."

"I know. He told me a little bit about it. Any idea where his father is?"

"To be honest, I don't know and I'm starting not to care. This has been a single-parent family for a long time now. You learn to adjust."

"I respect that. But a man should be there for his son."

"Oh! You have kids? How old?"

"Had. He passed away a few years ago."

"Oh my God, I'm so sorry!"

"Don't be. You didn't know. I understand that it can be hard."

"Yeah. When he left, claiming that he had some job to do, he promised that he'd take care of us. We haven't seen a penny. I'm afraid that we might lose the house."

"Drugs?"

"He's not a user… as far as I know."

"Dealer?"

"I don't like to think about it. I just want him here for Darius. He's lost without him."

My phone rang, "Excuse me." Buzzy had finished the deal early. He was calling me to come get him.

"I'm sorry to cut this short. I've got to go."

"I understand. It was nice to meet you, Mr. Black."

"I'm sure we'll see each other again."

She went to go check on Darius as I left. When I made my way out of the house, I passed a picture that was beside the door. It was Layla, in a wedding dress looking gorgeous, a much younger Darius, and…

"Hey, I like your wedding picture," I shouted to her from down the hall.

"Yeah, that's me and the baby-daddy in better times."

I stopped for a minute. "Alright then. Have a good one."

"You too."

It was Vic in the picture.

Shit.

Cost

I picked up Buzzy and we made our way back to the safe house. He seemed reluctant to talk about the deal. He was high as fuck though, so I assumed that it couldn't have been all bad. He didn't seem the least surprised about my encounter with Vic's family.

"Oh shit, nigga! Really? I knew he lived around here, but damn. Small world, ain't it?"

"What you mean you knew?"

I'll reiterate it: Never work with a junkie. It turned out that Buzzy had been familiar with Vic's situation. The two of us had spent the last few weeks staking out the pharmacy, but during the day that nigga was out getting high with Vic and Lenny.

He told me that Vic had been ducking a warrant that had just been put out for his arrest. Petty theft—minor shit—had he turned himself in, he would've served a few months and been out before Christmas. That stupid motherfucker let those two crackheads get in his ear and wound up snatching a purse on one of his drug-induced impulses. Who robs somebody in front of a fuckin' ATM? Amateurs never think about the cameras.

Turns out that Vic wasn't all that he was cracked up to be—pun not intended. He held it together well during the job but, according to Buzzy, he and Lenny had a thing for heroin. I didn't see the point in pressing Buzzy about it at that moment. I could worry about Vic and his family problems later.

"What did Carlos say?

"Man! He gave us the fucking hook-up!"

"Alright. Let's hear it."

"Okay. Check it. I walked in there right. I'm all like, 'Carlos!' And he's all like *Buzz Buzz!*—"

"Cut to the fuckin' punchline, Buzzy."

"Damn, negro! Quit actin' like we talking about freedom."

"Buzzy! Focus."

"He said that he'll give us twenty grand for the samples."

"I'm assuming that included the bag?"

"Yeah, nigga! We got more. Then after a little of my classic negotiation tactics, he said that he'll buy all the hard pills and codeine."

"How much?"

"Five racks a bag, but that's also if we throw in all the utensils, sterilizers, and shit like that."

"That's fine."

"Oh, and one more thing. Now before you get mad, just remember that he's the only one that can give us this kind of money upfront."

"What is it?"

"He has to pay us in installments. He said it's too much weight to move all at once. But he can buy one bag now."

"Aight."

"Word?"

On a normal day, I probably would've told Buzzy that Carlos and his cholos could go fuck themselves. Offering half of the value was a sign of disrespect. I'd give him his product for the money, but that'd be it. One bag of generics. It wasn't worth it to haggle. The fact of the matter was that we had to get rid of the shit, and five-hundred grand was a hell of a good jumpstart.

"Where's the twenty grand?"

Buzzy pulled up a brown paper bag and put that shit-eating smile on his face.

"Take ten. Leave the rest in the glove compartment. I think we've had enough for one day."

"Aight, man. So what's the plan now? Can I go back to my hoes and blows?"

"You can do what you want. I've got some running around to do."

I drove Buzzy back to his apartment complex. I didn't want to tell him too much more of the plan. I could tell he'd been lit up pretty heavy. He tended to run his mouth when he was that fucked up. I respected him for trying to hide it, but he was useless to me at the time. Besides, we both needed the rest. Ten grand would be enough to help me sleep right.

"Aight, Black, I'mma check you tomorrow."

"Buzzy! Don't die. I'll scoop you in the morning, around noon."

"Gotcha."

That motherfucker did the moonwalk all the way from the car to the door of his building. I ain't no snitch—but I called his momma to let her know that he'd be going in high. She wouldn't get on his case too much; she had her own problems. I just knew that she would also keep Buzzy in check, so he wouldn't overdose before the night was over.

I lit a cigarette and pulled off.

***

I couldn't sleep when I got home. I should have been happy. I just couldn't shake the thought of what Vic had put his family through. A month and a half is long time to be away from your kid. Now that motherfucker was in jail because of me. Fuckin' wife and kid were gon' be out on the street, while I lived the lavish life. The thought sickened me. The fuckin' sickness sickened me. I didn't want to be that guy. Not anymore.

I gave Vic the benefit of the doubt in my mind. Maybe he was just a victim of circumstance. Maybe he let those two idiots talk him into some dumb shit. No man could just walk out like that. Even at my worst, I never would've just up and disappeared. There had to be more to it. It could have just been a fuck up. We all fuck up sometimes. I thought that he might just need someone to give him a chance at redemption. I hoped he had a plan. Fuck, what if he didn't?

I laid there with my head spinning telling myself not to do it. It was fucking stupid, but I had to know. I had to help. I cleaned out my car, took a long shower, and sobered up the best I could.

Twenty minutes later I was on my way to the county jail where Vic had been sent and kept in holding while he awaited his trial. The drive was a while out, but when your conscience fucks with you that bad, you do anything to quiet it. I wasn't nervous. I just wanted to get it over with.

***

I got to the jailhouse just in time to sign in and wait for them to get to his name. When they finally got to *P*, they brought me and a couple of other families into the hall. I had about fifteen minutes to convince Vic to trust me with some sensitive information and give me his blessing to help take care of his family. I'd be out another couple of grand.

It was easy enough to lie to him. It was also necessary to make sure that he wouldn't have made some other contacts of his own. Whether or not he was locked up, guys like that have a way of getting their dirt done from behind the bars. I don't think he had any real reason to come after me. When's there's money involved though, you can't be too safe. If I was gonna do business in his hood, he had to agree to it. Jail cell or not, niggas get touchy over their territory worse than anyone.

"What the fuck are you doing here, Black?"

He wasn't exactly thrilled to see me. I knew that he wanted to make sure that he got his cut though. Most of the visitation rooms are usually tapped, especially the ones with temporary occupants. I wouldn't be able to go into too much detail, but I hoped he was street-wise enough to catch on to the subliminals.

"I wanted to talk to you about that *cake* we made."

"What about it?"

"I think we found some customers that like desserts."

"Which ones?"

"All of 'em. It's gonna take some time though."

"Shit. I got time. How much we talking?"

"Few weeks. Maybe a few months. It depends on how popular the bakery gets."

"Fuck the bakery. Where's my slice?"

"You'll get your piece of what's left."

"Fuck a piece. A third. That punk ass junkie opted out when he left with the eggs."

It was perfect. Lenny was still on the run—as far as I knew—and Vic thought he'd gotten away with half of the bags. It makes a little more sense why he gave up so easily. He'd thought that it was game over.

That asshole thought that Lenny had his half of the product. Who was I to correct him? When life gives you lemons, you trade them in for better fruit. I still had to seem like the neutral party, although the omission didn't do much to serve my guilty conscience. I still had to find a way to bring up his family. If it's out in the open, he wouldn't have a choice but to let me help.

"You'll get your share of what's left."

"You're a good man, Black."

"There's something else. You got a girl? A family to take care of?"

It was a softball way in, but I had to play this just right. The last thing I wanted was to be caught playing *good Samaritan* in some dude's home without his say-so. The expression on his face said more than I needed to know. Men with regrets get desperate. He couldn't hide his feelings much between his withdrawal shakes and junkie sweat.

"Yeah. We ain't exactly on the best of terms. It's a long story. They could use the dough though."

"Got an address?"

"I'll write it down for the guard. I don't trust any of these niggas around here. I don't need them running up on my house."

I didn't need the address, but if you're gonna bullshit, it's best to do it thoroughly. It's the best way to cover your own ass.

"Will do. I don't want you to worry about shit. You have my word that they'll be taken care of."

"There's something else, Black."

"What's that?"

"If anything happens to my wife or my son, I'm holding you directly accountable. I don't want you to get it twisted. It sounds like a threat—because it is—but it's also because I respect you. I know you'll do the right thing. Now, I'm not so worried, because you've got some incentive."

I didn't have anything to say to that. I understood what he was asking me. It was the no-choice ultimatum. It's a favorite technique that wannabe gangsters use when they don't have anything else to bargain with. It was effective for a sucker. The one problem was that I wasn't one. I'd have to deal with his overstep when he got out to keep him in line, but until then, he'd been beaten enough. I was never in it for the capital punishment.

I didn't have the time to be concerned. My intention was always to take care of his family and do the right thing by him for keeping his mouth shut. I even went out of my way to put some money on his commissary.

That threatening bullshit just rubs me the wrong fucking way. It always has. I gave him a low head nod and got up to leave. As I was making my way through the door he yelled to me, "Take care of my family, Black."

It was ten o' clock. I had a little over an hour to drive and, by the time I got in, I'd have about eight hours to sleep before it'd be time to set up everything for the deal with Carlos the next day. All I could think about was how worth it that it would be to finally be done with all this shit. And the irony of the whole situation. All I wanted was one last job to get away from that fuckin' life. Now, my only way out, was to dive deeper into it.

Momma always used to say, "The devil don't rent rooms. He sells real-estate." I was back on the damn market.

Deeper

I drove by Vic's on the way home, to make sure that everything was okay. I didn't stop in or anything like that. Layla had already left for work. If I did that, I would have scared the shit out of the little man. I could see him through his window playing video games. He was safe and didn't look like he was too bummed out by what had happened to him earlier.

I couldn't help but watch him for a minute or two too long. My son used to do the same thing. Laying on his stomach, with his head in the screen, playing some war-game like he could have been black Rambo. I always thought about him at the worst times. I still do. I pushed the memory down and pushed forward home, too tired for daydreaming.

When I left the facility where Vic was, they took my phone. I checked it a few times to make sure that I didn't miss anything important. To be honest, I was half expecting Buzzy to call me up on one of his "high-rants". I only had one missed call. I didn't recognize the number but they left a voicemail. I plugged it into the car speaker and listened to it on the drive.

You have... One... New Message. First Message:

"Yo, Black. I know that you ain't forgot about me, man. Buzzy told me that you and him did pretty good today. I'm glad to hear it. I'll be in touch with you soon to talk about when I'mma get my cut. You need to start picking up the phone—before I start thinking that you gon' pull some sly shit. You wouldn't wanna get the streets involved in this. I'll holla at you."

They hadn't caught Lenny yet. I didn't react. There was nothing to fucking react to. I just went home, took a few shots and knocked the fuck out. Sometimes you gotta wait for problems to come to you.

It's always best to wait peacefully.

***

I slept a little rougher than I had been. I'd hoped that clearing things up with Vic would do well to clean out my mind, but things had gotten exponentially worse. Now, instead of a guilty conscience, I had a laundry list of other people's shit to take care of. I thought about popping a pill, maybe two, but then I remembered that I still had to swing by Buzzy's and do the drop with Carlos. Lord knows what would've happened if we both showed up high as fuck. I thought it'd be better to see it through with a straight mind—headache and all.

I had already sorted the pills that Carlos had requested and threw a little less than our quote into a trash bag. I was used to having Buzzy there to plan out the details, but the tear that he'd been on made me lose a little faith in his restraint. The last thing we needed was an avoidable fuck-up because he wanted a fix.

I got to his place and parked in the lot. It was habit for me to go upstairs and say hello to his mother, but he had a loud mouth and didn't exactly live in the good part of town. I wasn't about to take the risk of leaving the drugs alone in the car and bringing them upstairs would've been stupid. Funny enough, it's the kind of shit that Buzzy would do.

I called him and told him that I was downstairs. He was barely paying attention. In the background all I heard was his mother complaining about Buzzy's mess and the clinking of glass against the floor. The motherfucker had lost his pipe. This was the wrong fucking time for that. I told him to bring his ass downstairs on the double. Carlos was waiting. There really was no reason to rush but, if he found his pipe, I'd be in for a long and stupid day of his bullshit.

When he finally came downstairs he looked suspicious. I don't like to call people on it, but business is business—it's always best to know what's going on in your partner's head. I'd have to be cool about it. If I let him talk long enough, he would say something that I could chime in on without it becoming a full-blown argument.

He didn't seem like his normal annoying self. He was quiet for the first half of the drive. I like to mind my business, but it's a huge red flag when someone is that silent before a deal. It suggests second thoughts. In this case, we didn't have the time for Buzzy's doubts.

"What is it, Buzzy?"

"Ah. It's nothing, man."

"You not back on that shit, are you?"

"No, motherfucker. I mean, kinda. What's it to you?"

"Look man, I don't give a fuck what you do to your own body, but do you really think it's a good idea right before a deal?"

"It ain't the fuckin' crack, man!"

"Then what is it? You know how I feel about the silent shit. Either you tell me what's up, or I swing back and drop you off. I can bring your cut around at like—"

"Nah. Nah. There's no need for that. Just some bullshit."

I had an idea of what the bullshit was as, if I'd gotten a call from Lenny, and he barely knew me, the chances were that Buzzy had gotten one too—probably along with an invitation to go to hell right along with him. I had to come clean. He would have never told me if I didn't. He ego-tripped anytime he was exposed as a liability.

"You get a call from Lenny too?" The way he looked, I knew that's exactly what it was. The only question I had was how the call went. Buzzy waited until we were outside of Carlos's to answer. He must've been afraid of my reaction.

"He threatened to kill my momma if I didn't give him half of my cut."

"What?"

"He blames me for the shit going wrong. Said he's trying to get out of town, and it's on me to help him make that happen."

"He blames you?"

"It was my blunt."

Buzzy had a problem with guilt. Along with his own special brand of bullshit, he had a bad habit of getting other people caught up in the mix with him. A lot of people saw him as a bad luck charm. I agreed, but we'd been friends since before he earned that title. I figured that I'd be immune—so long as I kept him off the shit whenever he was around me. I don't know why this particular time got to him so hard. It might have been the first time that anyone ever directly threatened his mom. We didn't have time for the therapy session. I eased his mind the best I could in the seconds before we got out of the car.

"Listen. We gon' head inside. We gon' make this money. After that, I got a few things that I gotta handle. I'll get back at you tonight and we'll figure out what we gon' do about Lenny. Sound good?"

"What if he serious, Black?"

"We'll handle it. Aight?"

He paused before he could collect himself.

"Aight. Let's go get paid."

***

It was a rare instance of a drug deal going that perfect. Buzzy loosened up as he watched me count through the banded hundreds. Carlos was actually a decent host. Like I said, "business respects business." He and I both appreciated the simplicity of a proper transaction; one where nobody's trying to fuck the other one out of anything.

We said our peace and made arrangements to make periodical drops to Carlos every two weeks or so. His clientele had been happy with the product—that meant that we should be in business until it was all gone. He even offered to pay us a *finder's fee* to keep our stash out of the hands of the competition. The plan was to sell a little on the side as needed but, for the most part, he had himself a deal. We could all get rich. No problems. No drama. Everything was back on track. Not counting a few loose ends.

"You gon' be aight taking an Uber home?"

"Nigga, what you mean? We just got paid! It's time to do it up like a Kardashian, man!"

I was glad to have him back to his normal, carefree self.

"I got some business to handle before all that."

"Well, fuck that. It's party time, my brother."

"Real shit, Buzzy."

"Aight. I'mma just kick it here then."

"You sure?"

"Yeah, man. Carlos is cool. You got the money. We gon' call over some *chicanas* and get our burritos rolled."

"Aight. Hit me up if you need anything. Try not to wake up in someone else's house please."

"I'mma be fine, negro. Vamanos."

I took a stack out of the bag and handed it over to Buzzy. I told him that I would give him the rest later. He didn't argue with me much about it. Even he was smart enough to know not to get high with more money on you than you're willing to lose. I warned him to stay away from the hard shit. There are better ways to go than an overdose. He'd already tangoed with that dragon enough times.

I left him there and did my best not to worry about it too much. I needed my mind to be as clear as possible. I wasn't sure exactly how I was going to present the situation to Layla. If I lied, and she found out, she wouldn't trust me to keep an eye on her and Darius. If I told the truth, same problem. I figured that, if I led with a handful of money to solve her problems, at worst she would be inclined to listen.

I parked in front of her house, took ten thousand out of the bag and put it in one of those giant yellow envelopes that Buzzy had the bright idea to steal along with the millions of dollars in narcotics. I had thought about clowning him for it, but here I was thanking God that I wouldn't have to have that much money out in the open. Cops patrol this neighborhood often. I decided to just chalk it up to being a "Buzzy blessing"; good things that happen for no reason.

I threw the bag with the rest of the money in the trunk and walked up to the door. Before I could even knock, it swung open.

Heart

"Hey! Vic told me that you'd be stopping by. Come in."

I was struck with silence. When you're shocked like that, it's best to just comply with the person that did it to you. I'm glad that Vic gave her a call, it saved me the trouble of making some shit up.

I followed her in and looked around to make sure that no one else was in the house. I'm not exactly sure what I was looking for, but I tend to trust my paranoia. I thought that I did it discreetly enough, but she noticed.

"Don't worry. It's just us. Darius is in the room playing video games."

"Uh…"

"He misses you, by the way. Says that you were gonna teach him to fight."

"Not exactly. I told him that he should take up boxing. Maybe pick a book sometime."

I didn't know how to feel. Anybody else on her end of the situation would be pelting me with all kinds of questions. She was acting as if I was just her neighbor and that everything going on was normal. I played along, knowing the tantrum would come sooner or later.

"Don't look so tense. There's some Hennessey in the kitchen if you want. Make yourself comfortable."

I poured two glasses and sat on the couch next to her. I didn't know how much Vic might've told her. At least she knew he was locked up, so I was grateful to be spared having to give that news. She walked over to Darius's room to close the door before joining me in the living room.

I still wasn't sure what her angle was. I actually started worrying that she might pull a gun out on me, out of pure frustration. The one time I left that shit in the car.

"So, is that for me?" she asked, pointing to the envelope.

"Yeah. About ten grand. It should be enough to help you keep the house."

When I handed her the envelope she started to crumble in the way that only a woman can. As if reality had put her in chokehold. It started with her eyes turning red, then shaking her head, and of course the lip quiver. I knew what was coming. I would have to be the fucking shoulder to cry on.

"He told me that he was done with this shit! He fucking promised, Black!"

"The man had to do what he thought was best for his family. Try to think about—"

"He didn't do what was best. He was selfish. He was always so fucking selfish!"

"How's that? The bills are taken care of. You're good. Darius is safe. What more could you want?"

I was playing with fucking fire, and I had no idea why. There's no way that shit could have ended well. She was looking for a target.

"Fuck the bills—I mean us. He told me that he would never put anything above *us*. Now he's in jail for God knows how long! What the fuck am I supposed to do?"

"Did he tell you about our arrangement? I've got you. You two don't have to worry about a thing. You don't even have to work if you don't want to. Anything you need, just call me."

"I can't ask you to do that, Black."

"You don't have to ask. I've already agreed to it."

"You have your own family to worry about. Your own things."

I made the classic mistake of putting all of my cards on the table just to play the hero. I'm still not sure if it was the brightest decision to make, but the past is done and the future will tell.

"Not anymore, I don't."

"Huh? Aren't you supposed to be this mad genius kingpin?"

"No. This bust was *it* for me. I've lost enough time. I've lost enough people. I've lost enough of myself. If I'm being honest, the only reason that I'm even here right now is because I don't want to see anyone else have to go through more pain because of me."

"It's not your fault, Black. You can't take on another man's burden."

"It doesn't matter where the blame falls. It was *my* job. If Vic's in jail because of it, the responsibility falls on me. It's how the real ones operate. Whether you like it or not this is what it is. If you stay hung up on the past, that's where you'll burn."

She took down both glasses of Hennessy and counted the money. Halfway through counting she started to cry again. I took it away from her and put it all the table.

"Maybe you should wait for that."

"And do what?"

"Pay your bills. Get something nice for yourself. It's the summertime. Go out and be a person. It's what I would do."

"I'm not you."

"That's even more of a reason to treat yourself. This doesn't have to be your fight."

"And who made it yours?"

It was like I was arguing with my girl again. Only she used to back down the second that I got too loud. Not Layla though. She wasn't a victim. If anything, she was just dealing with the repercussions of her past decisions. Sometimes it takes an echo for you to truly hear yourself.

Layla didn't need the money. Even if they did lose the house, she would be fine on the outside. She had heart, but it was her heart that was dying. She'd been fighting tooth and nail to keep it alive. We were alike in a lot of ways. I was ill-equipped for the argument, but I had an idea of what could save her from my fate.

"Do you and Darius have bathing suits?"

"Yeah."

"Well then, get dressed. We're going out."

She wiped her tears and the two of them got ready. I turned off my phone, needing some time away from the bullshit just as much as they did.

On certain days you just owe joy to yourself.

Souls

"Come on. Don't be a punk."

"Shut up! I'm not a punk. I'm just nervous."

"What are they gonna say...? 'Layla, come to work so we can take a look at that booty'?"

"Oh my God, Black, stop it!" she laughed.

"I'm just saying. It's not like you *need* to go."

"It just looks bad if I just call out like that. What do I tell them?"

"Just say that you're sick."

"I can't."

"You'll be fine."

I took both of them to the waterpark a few towns over. It seemed like something simple, but a few hours away from reality proved to be just what they had needed. It had been a rough few months for them. The next few would be easier, but were likely to be just as stressful, especially once the cops showed up to start asking questions. For the time being though, we didn't worry about that.

"Just call out. You're off tomorrow anyway. When's the last time that you treated yourself to a weekend?"

"Okay. Okay. Hold on."

While she handled her business on the phone, I turned mine back on to see if I'd missed anything important. I had a few voicemails, but no urgent texts, so I let them wait and rejoined Darius in teasing his mom about how nervous she was to take a personal day off from work.

"Black! She's doing it! She's doing it"

"Calm down, D. Let's see if she can knock this one out the park or not."

We made faces at her while we waited for her boss to pick up the phone. She thought it was amusing. Apparently it was entertaining enough to make her get over her nerves for the two minutes it would take.

"Hey, Vern, I'm having some family issues. I'm not going to be able to come in tonight... Okay. Understood. Thank you. I'll see you on Monday."

Just like that, a smile came over face. I couldn't hold mine back either. We pulled up alongside the house, and I unlocked the doors to let them out.

"And what do you think you're doing, Mr. Black?"

"I'm letting you guys out of the car. I've got some business to handle."

"Oh no you don't. I'm not gonna pretend to know what you do. But I'm guessing that you don't have to be there right now."

"Hmm. What's your point?"

"You make me call out of work. Now you want to leave me alone with nothing to do?"

"You got Darius."

I looked into the backseat of the car and saw that he'd fallen asleep not long after he'd just been bouncing around. I can't believe that I'd forgotten the signs of a tired child.

"Alright. You got me. A half hour."

"Deal. As long as you carry Darius's heavy ass into the house."

I woke him up and made him walk. He seemed happy to see me accompany them into the house. Once she put him to bed, she broke out her favorite wine, and we chilled out on the couch.

"Thank you so much for that. I'd forgotten how much fun a day could be."

"It's no problem at all. I enjoyed it too. You never realize how much you need to step out of life."

Our day at the park was oddly reminiscent of the lives that both of us thought we had at one point. We bonded over us both still chasing that fantasy.

Layla was an easy-going woman. She was never fond of the drama or the street life. She was one of those few lucky ones that were raised on princess movies and innocence. After a day with her, it's no wonder why Vic was able to scoop her so easily. Niggas like us know how to get the innocent ones. It was a bonus that they were gorgeous ninety percent of the time. Needless to say, we weren't taught to feel bad about it.

Even though she was a little younger than us, and despite her innocence, she learned the ropes of this life pretty quick. I guess it was a maternal thing. Once people have kids, they'll do whatever it takes to adapt and keep them safe. In a way I'm glad that things played out the way that they did. Layla was at the end of her rope. She didn't go into too much detail, but it's easy to tell when someone steps away from the metaphorical cliff. A taste of freedom can be a lifesaver.

"And so, I've just been doing what I can to stay sane. What's love got to do with it, right? I've got my son. I've got my home. Who am I to complain?"

"I suppose. You're definitely not wrong. But for the record, you have done a lot of complaining."

"Oh, shut up," she giggled.

We'd been flirting like that for a few hours. It was like we were two hormone-crazy high-school kids again. I only indulged in it because I never saw it going much further than words. I knew she liked me though. Stupid enough of me, I started to like her back. There was nothing else that I could do about it. The walls were down, and we'd been having a good time together. I stand by the idea that some emotions can't be ignored.

"What about you?"

"What do you mean?"

"Well, I've been here jabbering on about my life and times. What about you? How did you become the big, bad, man with an escape plan?"

"I honestly wouldn't even know where to start."

"How 'bout... How does a grown man, get a nickname like Black?"

It was the first time that anyone had asked me that question. Usually people just assumed that someone made it up and it stuck. I suppose that's the gist of it for most people, but mine actually had a story to it.

"You sure you wanna know?"

She threw her head into my lap and whispered, "Fascinate me." I was going to make something up, but we'd both been buzzed enough that I was pretty confident that she wouldn't remember a damn thing. Even if she did, I could always use the excuse.

"Alright."

***

Before I became the guy that was all about heists and other low-key shit, I had dreams of becoming the king of the city. I didn't give a fuck about rules, health, safety—none of that. I just wanted to have the best, sell the best, buy the best, and be the best at it. If it moved, I sold it. If it wasn't mine, I took it. I didn't let anything stand in my way.

I had the cars, the jewels, the hoes. Everything that any true gangsta could want. I damn near ran the city. There wasn't anything that went on without my say-so. I had power and my whole life was like a fucking rap video.

The problem with power and success is that they breed jealousy—and jealousy breeds competition. I went from being what essentially was a businessman to having to send some *unkind* messages to anyone that played games. I never counted, but a lot of people missed their birthdays because of me. I was hungry.

I wasn't into the traditional shit either. Anybody can pull off a drive-by or a stabbing. No, not me. That wouldn't have been good enough. I wanted my messages to send reverbs through the whole goddamn state. I needed people to fear me. Nothing spreads fear quicker than a man that people don't understand. So I went another route with it. I obviously dealt in your standard threats and chopping off body parts. But it proved ineffective after a while. On a simpler note, I just thought the shit was too messy. Too much evidence left lying around.

Instead I got creative. I'd gotten word from one of my boys about a bad batch of heroin being circulated in my part of town. The shit is always lethal, but it's not supposed to take out every motherfucker dumb enough to shoot it. We did the rounds. It took a while, but we got all of it off the streets. Best not to break your own people and shit like that. Rather than trash it, we intercepted a shipment coming in from the boys making noise. We traded their shit out with the "death batch". They had no idea what was coming.

Once their clientele started dropping dead, they had no business left. Word is, they even had their middle man killed. Collateral damage—he was in the coast guard; a decent guy. A few weeks after that, when their bank accounts started to hurt, they had no choice but to come to me.

I charged them double what the sacks were worth. They ended up having to cut it with a bunch of different shit just to see a profit. Their guys fell off one by one. I still don't think the people involved ever fully recovered their reputation.

They ended up merging with a guy who actually doesn't live that far from here. I killed their "American Dream", along with a few junkies that no one would ever notice was gone. In my mind it was the perfect offense. I lost some nights of sleep over it, but that's what this all leads to. Death. On one side or the other. It's always imminent.

They started to call me *El Destino Negro*. The Black Fate. A little while after that it was shortened to B.F. and once the homeboys got a hold of it, it became Black.

***

"Why *the Black Fate*?"

"Because it was synonymous with *The Terminal Disease*.

I wanted a name for myself, and I finally had it. I'd thought it was a warning for anyone that decided to try me. I was dumb enough to be slightly flattered. Buzzy had even convinced me that it was a sign of respect. As it turned out, it was the calling card of someone that they considered a dead man walking. They took their time taking their revenge.

"I'm rambling. You don't want hear any of this."

"No, No. I do. Please. Keep going."

"You sure?"

"Very. Just let me change real quick. And check on Darius."

"Good. I'm gonna need a little more to drink anyway."

"Pour two!"

I'd be lying if I said that I didn't enjoy her company. Besides, it had been so long since I'd spoken to anyone about it that it felt damn-near therapeutic.

"You ready?" I asked, when she came back into the room.

"Yeah. So you had the nickname. What happened? Did they ever try anything back?"

"Yeah. Unfortunately."

***

They started with Buzzy. They left him half-dead in the middle of the street when they couldn't find me. Needless to say I was ready to kill every motherfucker involved as quickly as possible. I *had* to before they got to me. I hunted for days. I put out foot soldiers. I did everything that I could to not have to deal with the anticipation and the waiting.

One night I was out on patrol. I got a phone call from one of my lower-level guys that someone had been circling my house. When I showed up, they sprayed my vehicle. I thought that it was weird that they'd missed me when I'd been so close. It was like they were intentionally hitting around me. I put it off on bad aiming. I shot back, but they'd gone too far and too fast for me have hit anything.

My girl was inside. She had just put my son, Tony, to bed and had laid down herself in our room waiting for me to come home. My little man saw my car pull up. He used to set up a chair and climb in front of the window to wave at me. I thought of that as they shot at my car. As soon as I knew that the coast was clear, I ran inside.

I found my girl holding our son in her arms. Shot five times: two in the head, one in the chest, two in the stomach. It was the first time I'd ever called the cops in my life. They put him in a body bag and questioned me, as if none of it mattered.

It goes without saying that I lost her. The last time that we saw each other was at his funeral. She couldn't even stand the sight of me. Shit. Can you blame her? I hated myself too. After that I went through a really bad drinking phase, and she went back to her painkillers. The entire relationship just kind of disintegrated.

I was lucky enough to have Buzzy to keep an eye on me. Had I been alone any of that time, I likely would have put a gun in my mouth and pulled the trigger. Even if I'd somehow fucked that up, my ex-girlfriend would have gladly finished the job. My fear of that didn't last long. She took herself out not too long afterward; intentional overdose.

Lucky for me, the hood tends to take care of its own, and no one—no matter how ruthless—appreciates it when an innocent kid is killed. He never admitted it, but I'm pretty sure that Buzzy led the charge on that one. He knows a few hardcore brothas that ain't too fond of child killers.

We caught the guys. They were just four young motherfuckers trying to make a name for themselves. I didn't even have to make the call. They were *dealt* with. No remorse and no retaliation. There's levels to the game, and they were playing with the wrong deck. The hood kept quiet and we all moved on.

Things settled down. But I was never the same. That was about five years back. I've been in and out of the shit ever since, tryna get out. I keep my own shit close to the chest though. Dominance of the hood belongs to a bunch of smaller sects now. I can get my beak wet from time to time but... I don't ever want to be *that* again. In that life, you're either setting yourself up for loss or for loneliness. I've had enough of both for a lifetime.

***

"Why'd you keep the name?"

"Black?"

"Yeah."

"The same reason Lucifer keeps his. It's humbling."

I expected that the reality of who I was would stun her. We often let our fantasies of a person take over when we want to know more about them. It was kind of my way of pushing down what I'd been feeling. I had a bad habit of pushing people away if I couldn't control them. I expected that to be the end of *us*. I wanted her to reject me. Instead, she poured another drink and leaned right into it.

"You know, you don't have to punish yourself."

"What do you mean?"

"People like us are soft at heart. We want to be strong. We think that if we build a tough enough exterior it can keep the world out. No world. No pain."

"And what's the problem with that?"

"The pain ends up being the only thing that we ever let in. When you're broken, it's the only thing that you tend to trust."

I'd never thought of that before. Even if it ever had come across my mind, I was always more focused on how to move forward and how to move on. There was something about that moment though. That revelation. I couldn't turn off the thoughts.

As the rain came down hard as rocks on the windows, I tried to force myself to leave, but my legs wouldn't let me.

"Have you ever forgiven yourself, Tony?"

"It's Black."

"No. It's Tony. I don't want you mixing me up in your head with all the worst thoughts of yourself."

"Fair enough... Just don't call me that in public. It might look bad."

"Do I look like a give a damn about any of that?"

She slid her hand over to mine and stared deep into my eyes. I had to get out. A smart man would have gotten out.

"I should go."

"Really? It's raining cats and dogs. We've been out all day. And how many drinks have you had?"

"I'll manage."

"Don't be ridiculous."

She grabbed a blanket from her bedroom and cuddled up beside me. I don't know what I was thinking, but liquor has a way of making dumb things seem like a good idea.

"Come on. I don't bite. Besides, it's freezing in here."

We made it about five minutes into a movie, then moved to the bedroom.

The storm was enough to keep Darius from hearing the sounds of her orgasms.

I don't regret it.

Back to Bullshit

The next morning was like something pulled straight from a nineties sitcom. I woke up a little earlier than everyone else. Smoked a cigarette and then started on breakfast. Layla and Darius had gotten so used to barely getting by that I thought that it would be a nice gesture. As the eggs cooked, Layla was woken up by the smell. We didn't say two words to each other. She just walked up in her oversized T-shirt and hugged me from behind.

We were worried about how it might look to Darius. Surprisingly, he was more interested in a hot meal first thing in the morning. I forgot how simple it was to start the day off right when the people in your life care about you. I made us all plates, we turned on the television and for a brief time everything felt right again.

But we all had to come back from our fantasies. The fact of the matter was I still had drugs to sell, a loose end to cut, and now I had to figure out how to get out of here without too many people noticing or getting suspicious.

"Lay, have you seen my phone?"

"Oh yeah, it's in the room on the dresser. I put it on the charger for you."

As soon as she said that, I could hear the constant vibrations from the notifications. The damn thing sounded like it was gonna explode.

I had about forty missed calls. All at once the pressures of life returned to me. I didn't even bother taking a shower. I just got dressed and shot to the front door. It's never a good idea to step out of your life when you're as deep in things as I was. It was as if the last twenty-four hours never happened.

"Wait. Where are you going?"

"I've just got to handle some business. I'll come by a little later to check on you guys."

"Okay… You sure you okay?"

I wasn't. Most of the calls had been from Buzzy and he also went out of his way to leave me half a dozen voicemails. Buzzy barely let the phone ring twice before he tried to call you again. The only reason that he would call that much is if some shit went down that he didn't know how to handle. The high volume of missed calls was normal for him.

What bothered me was the voicemails. The last time that he left me a voicemail was to let me know that someone had just been put in the ground for me. Any others that I'd ever gotten were just more bad news.

I kissed Layla goodbye. In retrospect, I should've gone without doing that, but I couldn't help myself. I was falling in love with a taken woman. I thought that had things gone south, which I expected them to, I wouldn't be alive long enough to have to deal with the repercussions anyway.

I tried to justify it to myself by thinking that I'd just missed that level of intimacy. The truth was—it wasn't any of the bullshit. It was her. She was the woman I was looking for, and those few minutes that we spent together that morning would fuel every decision that I would make after that.

I wanted that back. I wanted that forever. I would do anything that I could to make sure that I felt that again. Needless to say, my plans changed.

"Just do me a favor and be safe, Tony."

I promised her that I would. It was a lie but there was no other way.

***

I plugged the phone into the car and listened to the voicemails as I drove back to the safe house to check on the drugs and grab a few more guns. If everything had gone according to plan that day, I would need all that I could get.

You have... Five... New Messages. First Message:

"Yo Black. It's Vic. I need to talk to you. I think I got a way to get out of here on the level. Come by on the next visitation day. Remember to bring some cash for me. My commissary running low."

I didn't really give a fuck about *him* at the moment.

Next Message:

"My main man, Black! It's the B to the U to the Z... Z... Y... hit me up, man. Trina and these THOTS over here on twenty-fourth wanna see how us real niggas do! It's time for a fiesta, man! Ayyy!!! We want some puss... aye—"

Message Erased. Next Message:

"Ay! Black. You already know who it is. I need my cut. Meet me at Buzzy's ASAP."

They still hadn't caught that motherfucker, Lenny.

Next Message:

"Tony. It's Buzzy's mom. He didn't come home last night. He promised me he would. He's never late like that without calling. Please see if you can find him and tell him to come home. I hope you boys aren't out there getting into any trouble."

His mom was sweet. She over-worried. Funny thing is, she actually did have colitis. I don't think Buzzy really gave a fuck though. He just said that when he was scared shitless. I never asked him if it actually worked.

Next Message:

"Mr. Boykins, good evening. This is Amy calling on behalf of New City University Hospital in regards to a Mr. Christopher 'Buzzy' Busey. Mr. Busey has suffered a couple of on and off seizures following a non-lethal alternation with the New City Police Department. We've tried to contact an immediate family member, but your number was the only one that he would give us. If you could please come down to the hospital to fill out some paperwork it would be highly appreciated as more information is needed to continue his treatment. Feel free to call us back at—"

Message Erased. End of New Messages.

Fuck.

I guess that it was still better than an overdose.

***

I got off of the road heading home and got onto the highway. The hospital wasn't far, but I knew that I'd have blown through a few traffic lights and broken some other laws while I was at it if I had stayed on the main road. I was pissed the fuck off and worried at the same time.

Had the cops not locked him up yet, with the way that Buzzy used he'd still be withdrawing pretty bad. New City was a decent place, but they didn't have the patience for junkies. They usually just put them to sleep and let them sweat it out in the emergency room. I needed to count on a lot of things to go right for shit to work out without a problem.

It's like no matter how close I got to peace, the devil was right there playing goalie and kicking me back into play. I was more down for this final round of bullshit. You never want to get the best out of a hood-soldier, you give him something to fight for. I now had plenty.

When I got to the hospital, I didn't even bother going through the front door. If I would have done that, there'd be a record of my visit. You never want there to be paper trail of where you've been bouncing around to. I parked across the street and ran right to the emergency room. It's always chaos in there, but I had a hunch of where Buzzy would be. The hospital, for lack of better words, was fairly segregated. I started my search with the rooms in the back.

I found him at the end of the hall. He was guarded by two armed officers. I'd been known around the precincts, but it was always because of a third party—usually for shit like this. I got a pass from one of the nurses. It's easy enough, and they don't make you sign in. Besides, I was his emergency contact, which meant my name had to be on the list. They didn't give me a hard time getting in. As a matter of fact, they were probably excited. A few of the officers down at the station would give an arm and a leg just to pin some shit on me.

He was sweaty, covered in bandages, and hooked up to an I.V. It was hard to fucking see but, even at a moment like that, I was hopeful that it would be just the kick in the ass that he needed to get him to quit the shit for good.

The doctor came by and told me that he'd been in a state of delirium and would be in and out of consciousness. I took the free minutes to try and check up on Layla and Darius. I didn't think much of it when she didn't pick up. At least someone was having a more productive day.

I was relieved when he finally woke up

"Ah. Where the fuck you been at, negro?"

"I told you that I was gonna be busy. How you feeling?"

"I think I pissed myself, Black."

"I'm pretty sure that's an understatement."

"What?"

"You smell like you look."

"Sexy?"

"Nah. Like shit."

"Fuck you, man."

"It's good to see you up."

"Ain't good to be up. How bad is it?"

"You tell me. Looks like you got your own personal security."

When he saw the officers outside of his room, the jokes stopped. I don't think I'd ever seen Buzzy cry until that day. A man only shows his true colors when the law finally catches up with him.

"Shit. They got ol' Buzz this time. I'm sorry, Black."

"Sorry? What happened! What did you do?"

Around the time he called me, he ran into Lenny on the street. Apparently the two of them had the night of their lives courtesy of Buzzy's wallet.

After a few hours getting high and fucking around with some prostitutes, the two of them got the bright idea to rob the local corner store. When the cops showed up, Lenny booked it through the streets and left Buzzy to fend for himself with a bag of weed in his pocket.

"At least it wasn't the shit you put in your veins."

"That's not the worst of it though. The reason we were robbin' the bodega is because Lenny needed the money. He's tryna get out of town."

"What's that got to do with me?"

"He asked for you specifically. When I told him that I didn't know where you were, he threatened to kill my momma if I didn't roll."

"You gotta stop going for that, man. Do you know where he's at now?"

"I got an idea."

As I was leaving the hospital, some detectives turned into Buzzy's room. He had priors, but the shit that they caught him with was a misdemeanor at worst. He'd be going away for a while. I hoped it'd be just long enough for him to get clean.

When Lenny pressed him, Buzzy gave Lenny the address to the safe house—hoping that I would be there to take over the bullshit. I was pretty sure that's where he'd be. It'd been a few hours. I didn't have any more missed calls. More than likely he'd gone straight to the house thinking that he could lay low there.

That'd explain the frantic voicemail.

***

I called Layla on my way to the safe house and told her to take Darius to the movies. I'd left them enough money to stay out for the day. I promised that I'd be back around dinner time and I honestly just called to hear her voice. I wanted to make sure that the two of them were safe before shit got rowdy.

Just as I expected, when I got to the house, the side window had been broken into and the television was on full blast. On top of everything, this motherfucker was stupid enough to leave the door unlocked. When I got in, he was laid out on the recliner with a gun on his stomach, watching a news report about himself.

"Tonight on Eyewitness News: Career criminal Leonard McDowell still at large after a four day manhunt. Officers reported to have last spotted McDowell in the area. He is believed to be seeking associates for his inevitable fleeing of the state. We're told that officers are operating under the assumption that this is in some way connected to the burglary at Gold's pharmacy just three days ago. Officers urge community cooperation; and as always, if you see something, say something..."

"I look good on the ol' box here, don't I, Black?"

"You look crazy. What the hell are you doing here? Thought you'd be halfway across the globe by now."

"Funny thing about that, it turns out it's hard to leave the country when you've got no money."

"Didn't you steal enough from Buzzy?"

"It was my fucking cut, Black! And not even all of it. Word is, we've got a matter of five million to attend to."

"Did Buzzy also happen to tell you that we're still trying to unload most of this shit?"

"As a matter of fact, he did. That's why I went looking."

I walked through the apartment with my hand on my gun just in case Lenny decided to bring some goons along with him for an easy score. Everything was tossed all around and he left a ton of my shit broken. When I checked in the bedroom, my jewelry and pocket cash were gone, but it didn't look like he'd noticed the shifted tile under the bed. Once I knew that the drugs were safe, I told him to stand and checked him for a wire.

"You ain't gonna find nothing, man. They don't offer deals to guys like me. I've had 'em lookin' for days. Even for the guy on the run, that's embarrassing."

"Was it necessary to turn my place upside down?"

"What was I supposed to do, wait for you to finish gallivanting around town? Time is of the essence, motherfucker."

"But you got time to sit on my couch, drink my liquor, smoke my weed and watch yourself on the news…"

"Don't be an asshole, Black. I've come with a proposition."

The proposition was bullshit. He couldn't find the drugs, so he needed me to hand them over to him. The guy was a little shorter, a lot lighter, and had been on drugs since before he was fucking. He wouldn't have been able to use force without a gun. And I was surprised that he'd still held onto his piece. I figured he would have sold it for a quick high. It would have explained why he wanted to rob an old man's corner store.

"So what do you say? Vic's in jail. Buzzy about to be locked up too. Five million two ways ain't a bad deal. Not to sound any kind of way, but it'll also get me outta your hair. Think about it, Black. The one man in a million-dollar heist that leaves unscathed."

"And for what reason would I do that? How do you know that I won't call the cops right now?"

"Because you're a hood nigga, Black. All that high-mind, education, logic bullshit don't fly with guys like us. You're thinking the same thing that I'm thinking. Cut the loose ends and leave with profit."

"You're not wrong about that."

"Exactly. You know Carlos?"

"I've heard of him."

"We make the drop. Get the cash and I'm out of your hair just like that."

"And exactly what happens if I say no?"

"Well, it's not like I don't know where you sleep. Besides, do you really want to go toe to toe with a guy that has nothing to lose?"

"Do you?"

"My man, Black! Buzzy told me that you wasn't nothing to fuck with."

"He's right."

"Well, neither am I."

Lenny pulled the old revolver from out of his jeans, cocked it, and shot the wall right next me. When I grabbed my ringing ears he gut-checked me with his elbow. He stepped over me when I fell to the floor.

"WHERE ARE MY FUCKING DRUGS, BLACK!"

I had to play the next few minutes carefully or he'd blow my head off before I even had the chance to collect my thoughts. I pointed to my car outside. I'd left the bag of money in there from the day before. It was a small trade in exchange for my life.

I pulled the car keys from my pocket and handed them to him. He put on a hoodie and searched the car until he found the money in the trunk. For a second I'd hoped it'd be enough to send him on his way for good; I could always recoup the loss from my bi-weekly drop with Carlos. He grabbed the bag and came back in the house.

"Good boy, Black. Now where are the drugs?"

"Carlos."

"Carlos? The fuck you mean?"

"I had Buzzy drop off the bags there. We're supposed to collect on it tomorrow night."

"Well, how the fuck you gon' do that with Buzzy in jail?"

"I didn't know. But I got you now. If we head over there, we can make the exchange. You can take your money and get the fuck out of town."

"Hmm. Sometimes all it takes is a little ass-whooping for a nigga to get right. It's good to have you back to your senses."

He helped me up, we shared a drink and talked about our game plan. I entertained his nonsense stories until my ears finally stopped ringing. After a while of some *bonding time,* I got a call from Layla. I didn't pick it up, but I took the opportunity to get the hell out of there.

"What you mean you gotta go?"

"Man, they got Buzzy and Vic. The whole damn country is out looking for you. It's only a matter of time before they pin some bullshit on me. The *last* thing that I'm gonna do is help them out by switching up my schedule."

"...Aight. Be back here before the drop tomorrow."

"You got it."

"Don't make me come looking for you, Black!"

"Never even crossed my mind."

It was a risk, but it worked. I grabbed my car keys and headed over to Layla's. I called her back on the drive over. It was a welcome shift in reality. Darius had gotten into another fight. This time they actually got his chain.

Strategy

"Where is he, Lay?"

"He's in his room. He's really upset... Is that blood on your lip?"

"Yeah. Don't worry about it. I'm fine."

"Tony, tell me what happened."

"I will. But don't make me lie to you right now."

"Okay. I'll get you some ice."

"Thanks, baby."

It slipped. She was a bit frazzled by the pet-name, as was I. It didn't matter in the moment. I could hear Darius crying through the door. I knocked.

"Darius! You alright, little man?"

"Go away, Black!"

"I will. As soon as we talk."

He was quiet for a little too long. When I opened the door, I saw him in the middle of the floor, trying to figure out how to load a gun that Vic had given him some months back. I knew that I had to keep it calm. If I scared him away at that time, I'd never be able to get through to him again.

"What's that?"

"Mine. You can't have it!"

I closed the door behind me and locked it. If Layla knew about this, she'd probably lose her fucking mind. It's what a *normal* parent would do anyway. Lucky for Darius, my methods were unorthodox.

"I don't want it. I've got a few of my own. It looks like you're having some trouble there."

"It's jammed."

"Mind if I take a look at it?"

He handed me the gun. When I removed the clip, I saw that it wasn't jammed—it was empty. At least someone was responsible enough not to give him bullets. When I showed him, I could tell he was embarrassed. I gave it back, and he asked me if I'd ever killed anyone.

"A few people. Only because I had to. But you see, this…" I took the gun from him and placed it on his desk, "…should always be a last resort."

"So how am I supposed to get my chain back?"

"That's a good question. If I was *my* father, I'd tell you 'by not getting it taken in the first place' and then make you do some push-ups. Do you want to do some push-ups?"

"No."

"Well, in that case, you've got to use your mind, little man."

I was happy to see that I piqued his interest.

"You see, the guy that took your chain, he only did that because he's scared of you. You pose a threat, so he needed something to show everyone around that he thinks he's tougher than you. But, he only *thinks* it. If he believed that for real, he would've never had to take your chain in the first place. Which means what?"

"He's still afraid."

"He's even more afraid. Because now, you have a reason to become everything that he fears most. He just sealed his own fate, and he doesn't even know it."

"So how do I get it back?"

In Sun Tzu's *The Art of War* he speaks of deception, preparation and cleverness. "The competent general never appears to be so." When I explained this to Darius, I could see his imagination flourish. When I tried to hand him his gun back, he slid it under his bed and started writing.

If Lenny wanted to play games, I was more than happy to oblige him. All of the pieces were already in place. He'd confused brawn for intellect.

***

Layla overheard my conversation with Darius and decided that it'd be best for her to wait outside the door with the bag of ice. I left him in higher spirits, but I'd also managed to make her worry. I hoped that she wouldn't ask me what I knew she was going to. When I left Darius's room, she was leaning on the wall with her head down.

"Are you okay?"

"I'm fine."

"You know what I have to do right?"

"I know enough to know that you're not a hundred percent sure that you'll be coming back after today. "

"That means you also know that I wouldn't do this if I didn't have to."

"I'd like to believe that."

I put my hand on her cheek and lifted her face up. I promised her that I would be back and that we would all go on vacation together. I kissed her and her eyes started to water.

"Do you trust me?"

"I'm trying"

We made love that night as if we would never see each other again. I prayed, for the first time in years, hoping that God would let me keep my word.

***

"Tony!"

I'd just fallen asleep that morning when Layla screamed my name. I put on my pants and grabbed my gun. Waking up to screams is never good a sign.

"Come on, Black. Bring your ass out here!"

I hadn't even heard Lenny break in. Layla had gone into Darius's room to wake him up for breakfast. When she opened his door, Lenny had him tied up to his chair and was pointing a gun to his head demanding to see me.

"Tony! Do something."

I was frozen. In an instant I saw the entire life that I'd hoped for shatter. All I could think about was my son. I would've done anything he said to keep Darius safe. I couldn't stand the thought of another one being killed because of my bullshit.

"Lenny, what the fuck are you doing?"

"Me? What the fuck are you doing? Shacking up and playing house with Vic's girl. You know they kill motherfuckers for a lot less, nigga."

"Would you put that fucking gun down! You're scaring him."

"Oh, Black, nothing would make me happier. The only problem is, my price just got higher. That is, unless you want a hit on your back on top of two dead bodies to explain to the cops."

"Lenny. Cut the shit! You'll get your money; put the gun down!"

"Well, as long as we got a deal. Now, be a peach and tell me where the rest of the drugs are."

"They're not here."

"Where the hell are they?"

"I'll tell you out there. Now put the fucking gun down!"

"You're a shrewd negotiator, Black. But alright, I'll put it down."

He shot me twice in the leg. I fell against the wall.

"Now that I've got some reassurance. Let's go!"

He aimed the gun at me while I hobbled over to the front door. As we made our exit, I bled onto the wooden floor panels. It was a decent amount, but nothing lethal. I'd have to adapt my plans for the injury. As I was leaving I told Layla that I was sorry.

We got in the car. Lenny made me drive. He got in the backseat and ducked low to avoid being seen; still pointing the gun at my lower spine, he ordered me to take him to the drugs. I didn't have much of a choice. I had to play the next few hours pitch perfect or die trying to.

I got a call from Buzzy sooner than expected. Lenny was hesitant to let me answer it, but when I told him who it was, it piqued his curiosity. He grabbed the phone from me. I'd only heard half of the conversation, but Lenny redirected me to a busted down deli just north of town.

The last thing he asked was for Buzzy to grab the bags and meet us at the deli.

"Apparently brother-man Buzzy got off on a police brutality case. Hit the freeway. It's about to be raining money all over this damn place."

I just hoped that Buzzy would get the note that I'd left in the safe house.

Snitch

We got to the restaurant just in time to watch Buzzy nervously walk in. I knew that something was up. When you have officers guarding your hospital room, it most often meant that you were going down for some big shit. There was no way that they'd let him off that easily without him striking some sort of deal.

I used a T-shirt that I'd left in the car to cover up the wound and got out of the car. Lenny stayed behind. He was too afraid of someone spotting him to do much more than fill my head with his empty threats.

I'm not sure if he noticed the plainclothes officers sitting in the car just a few parking spots away. I knew that they noticed me though. Undercover cops do a shit job at hiding their intentions at the spur of the moment. I made a point to cause a bit of a scene on my way inside. I held my leg and took my time limping to the restaurant door. Once I'd made the wound obvious, there was no taking their eyes off of me. For the time being, I was safe.

Buzzy and I had never been to that particular place before, but we'd always had a plan of what to do, just in case either of us were ever in a situation like this one. He sat in a booth with his back against the wall and darted his head around looking for me. He seemed a little more stable than the last time I'd seen him. I figured that they'd let him have his fix, just to get through the sting.

There was no doubt in my mind that he was wearing a wire. When I saw him I made sure to play up the injury the best that I could. I thought that if I could convince the officers that I was an unwilling participant, it would keep them from arresting me. As long as I could hold off that *game-over* moment, the ball was still in play and I still had a chance to make it home. Our code phrase was *you fit?*

"Buzzy!"

"What's going on, Black? What the fuck happened to your leg?"

"Just a little mishap. Nothing too serious."

"Where's Lenny?"

"He sent me alone. Good enough for him. I'm pretty sure he's trying to break the record for the longest time *at large.*"

"Shit, man. Well, that motherfucker got me into some deep shit."

"Deep shit, how? You fit?"

"Yeah man, I'm good. I'm just worried about how we gonna move the rest of the bags."

"That's y'all deal, man. I told you that I'm out of all this shit."

"You ain't gonna do the drop?"

"I wasn't. The motherfucker basically has a gun to my head."

"So what's the plan?"

"As of now, we eat, we ride back, and we play it by ear from there."

"This whole thing is really fucked up, Black. I don't think I want to do this shit anymore either."

"Well, if everything goes as I think it will, you may not have to."

"The last thing my momma saw me do was stick a fuckin' needle in my arm and run off with the son of a bitch that put me on the radar. I can't let that be her memory of me. Whatever happens, don't let me die, Black. I mean that. *Whatever*, happens. Don't let me die without saying goodbye to my momma."

"You have my word, Buzzy."

We ordered two burgers and a pot of coffee. We'd always agreed that if we were lucky enough to have a last meal together, that's what we'd get. I don't know how much he *actually* believed that I had some magical power that would keep him alive. It seemed to comfort him nonetheless.

We ate in silence for the rest of meal. I could tell that the officers were getting impatient, but we still had about an hour to kill before I would be sure that Carlos was awake and sufficiently drunk. He was known as a sharpshooter. I didn't need any of that spoiling my plans.

We left the restaurant and Buzzy got into the passenger seat. He wasn't as surprised as I was to see Lenny. The undercovers followed us about seven car-lengths back. Buzzy and I were the only ones that noticed.

***

Lenny had already been celebrating in the backseat. Those kind of niggas always like to count their chickens before they hatch. In his defense, I guess you could say that it was the most obvious way to interpret the situation. At least I'd hoped.

"Where the fuck are the bags, Buzzy!"

"Damn, Lenny, calm down. Carlos got 'em."

"Carlos!"

"Yeah, nigga. Ain't Black tell you?"

"Yeah, I told him."

"Both of y'all need to shut the fuck up right now!"

He pointed the gun at Buzzy.

"Aight, Buzzy. No more fuckin' around. I actually like you, man. If I find out that you're up to some shit with this nigga over here, I'll put ya ass in a box right next to him."

"Reebok or Nike?"

"Motherfucker!"

Buzzy kept him distracted enough in nonsense for me to send a quick text message to Carlos, letting him know what was coming. Buzzy and I just had to seem incompetent enough that Lenny wouldn't have a choice but to join us inside.

"Buzzy."

"Aight, Black, you right. Ay, Lenny."

"What?"

"I was just fucking with you, man. My bad. I get all nervous and shit during jobs like this. It happens all the time. Did you know my momma had colitis?"

"What the fuck?"

"I ain't bullshittin'! It gets all up in your colon right—"

"Black, I'mma kill this motherfucka if he don't shut the fuck up."

"Both of you relax. We're here."

Lenny checked his clip and crept up from the backseat.

"Just like old times, huh, boys?"

"Yeah. With the added benefit of a gun to our heads."

"I was never planning on shooting either one of you. And Black, I hope that there's no hard feelings, my brother. I just had to prove a point. Look at us now! We all about to get this money and have the streets on fire."

He patted me and Buzzy on the shoulders as he was getting out of the car. He took his time looking around. Lucky for us, the detectives had been wise enough to park around the block. He had no idea what was about to happen.

Buzzy gave me the look, and I reached under the seat to grab the extra glock I kept on me. I was surprised that Lenny hadn't noticed it. I guess that I've got Buzzy to thank for keeping him distracted. People are easy to manipulate in stressful situations.

We got out the car, and Buzzy led us into Carlos's house with his usual cholo battle cry.

"Aye, my friends! *Voy con el fuego!*"

I started my mental countdown.

Break

"Where the fuck is he at?"

"Relax. He said he'll be here. We just gotta wait."

When Buzzy went to knock on the door, there was no answer. We waited for him to go in and check. Once we were sure that the coast was clear, we went in the house. No one was home, but it looked like whoever had been just left; there was still a blunt burning on the table.

Lenny directed us to the couch and told us to wait there while he searched for the money.

"Either one of you motherfuckers move and I'll put a bullet in your fuckin' head."

Buzzy started getting nervous and figured he'd roll himself something to calm his nerves. It was laced, but that's how Buzzy smoked it.

"So what happens now?"

"Now we wait for your boys to come and save our asses."

"How in the hell we gon' do that?"

"Don't you got a panic button?"

I looked outside and there was no sign of the guys that had been following us.

"Or plan B."

"What's plan B?"

Carlos and his goons pulled up to the driveway a few seconds later. I told Buzzy that when shit hit the fan to hit the ground or make a run for it. When the guys got out of the car, Carlos wasn't with them. That put us at a bit of a disadvantage.

They'd seen my car parked out front and the front door left open and armed themselves.

"Ay, Lenny! We got company!"

"The fuck you mean?!"

Lenny peeked through the window and his face turned white.

"Where the fuck is Carlos?"

They must've seen him. The last thing I heard before the chaos were the sounds of glass shattering and Buzzy and Lenny hitting the floor. I was still bleeding out pretty bad, so I had to be careful with my next few moves.

The gunfire attracted the attention of our escort officers who bulleted down the road with their siren on, hoping to stop the gang from spraying the house from top to bottom. All they succeeded in doing was redirecting the gunshots to themselves. AK-47s were no fucking joke, and definitely not street legal; they distracted with each other while Buzzy and I dealt with Lenny.

"Where's my fucking money, Black?!"

He rolled around on the floor screaming with the gun in his hand. I don't know where he was hit, but he was, which would make all of this easier. I hopped over and dropped my elbow onto his head. When the gun fell from his grip, Buzzy grabbed it and aimed it at him as he sprawled out bleeding from his nose.

"I swear to God, I'mma kill you, Black."

"Nigga, shut the fuck up before I kill *you.*"

Pain can do some unspeakable things to a man if he doesn't prepare himself for it. Lenny's mistake was a lack of preparation and underestimating the enemy. I'd have to remember to teach Darius the same lesson. It's never good to be the guy that falls for anything.

As the goons had their back and forth outside with the cops, Buzzy and I did our best to dodge the stray bullets that pierced the windows every few seconds.

"What do we do, Black?!"

"As of now we've got to wait!"

"Wait for what?!" Buzzy screamed.

A river of sirens flooded the block to back up the two officers. I crawled over to the front door and locked it before they could attempt to retreat in the house. One by one the cops took them out until the last guy surrendered. They still popped him in the shoulder just to send a message to any gang-bangers that might be watching and getting some bright ideas.

When the bullets stopped I signaled to Buzzy as I crawled over to the door that led to Carlos's basement. When he saw where I was heading, he knew the plan.

"You think you big shit, Black?!" Lenny screamed.

I'd almost forgotten about him. He'd been such a big problem just a half hour earlier.

"You think these motherfuckers won't come for you? You think this shit is over, Black? The streets forgive a lot of shit, but they ain't gonna forgive this. And if they don't get you, Vic's gonna have your head on a motherfuckin' pike. And Buzzy, if you think that I forgot—"

Buzzy let off two rounds into Lenny's head and dropped him cold mid-sentence.

"That motherfucka was getting ready to threaten my momma again."

"Thanks, Buzzy. I was gonna get to that."

"You wasn't gettin' to shit. What we doing?"

We crawled down to the basement, and I showed him the tunnel that Carlos had used to smuggle in some of his product. It also doubled as a convenient little escape route just in case he ever got caught slipping.

"It leads about two blocks out."

Buzzy smiled, and then his expression dropped. I wanted him to come with me.

"I can't do that, Black. I've already got this shit." He pulled his wire off of his chest. "I've got a deal to get out in a year, and I just killed that motherfucker upstairs."

"It was self-defense."

"Self-defense or not, reality is reality. If I don't go now, they'll be gunning for me the same way they were for homeboy upstairs. They've heard enough for you to get the hell out of here. I'm wrapped up, man. I don't have any more energy for this shit."

"So what are you gonna do?"

We heard the sound of an air horn. The cops that had been handling Buzzy demanded that he come out with his hands "to the sky".

"I'mma go upstairs. Finish that blunt and try to come up with a story about how I just coughed and the gun went off."

It was hard to hold in the laugh. I think his intention was to lighten the moment.

"I'll do what I can to cover your ass, man. But, you gotta go before they have both our asses out there with Vic."

"Aight, Buzzy."

I took off through the tunnel. The last thing that I heard Buzzy scream as a free man was, "Take care of my momma, Black! You know she got colitis!"

I got to a ladder that led to a false sewer top. When I climbed out, I was a block away from Layla's. The shirt that I'd tied around my leg had fallen off during the gunfight. I was still bleeding heavily. It was hard to walk, even harder to see straight.

***

The hood has a way of protecting its own. There were a bunch of people who watched the war taking place outside of their windows. I know that a few of them had to have seen me. I didn't care, I just needed to get to Layla's. I needed to get back home.

When I got to the door, it seemed that she was waiting for me. I hadn't even noticed the cameras outside at Carlos's. She was watching the entire thing go down on the news. She hugged me and gasped, terrified when she saw how much blood I'd lost.

"Darius, go get some towels and my first-aid kit from the bedroom!"

"But—"

"Now!"

She laid me on the couch. I was drifting in and out of consciousness, but I made sure to keep myself awake long enough to see the end of the news report.

"Tragedy on the East Side this morning as officers confront what appeared to a faction of the ruthless Latin gang known as SK-5s. Officers engaged in a firefight with the gang after an anonymous tip led them to the home of a local resident where the body of recently deceased suspect Leonard McDowell was found with two bullet wounds to the head. Officers have refused to comment on the presence of McDowell in the exchange, though in a statement they claim that, "All residents of New City can sleep at ease tonight." This was truly a spectacle to behold and a major redemption for the once-alleged incompetence of the New City Police. More on this story as it develops."

Everyone wanted it to be over. You could almost hear the unanimous sigh of relief. I was happy to see that they hadn't mentioned Buzzy in the report. It meant that he may still have some pull. At the very least, his deal was still intact and he wouldn't have to worry about doing too much time.

Layla turned the channel so as not to worry Darius too much. At his age, kids tend to know more than they let on. He was bright enough to know that I had something to do with it all. It's good respect though. Don't trip on it.

As Layla picked the shards of the bullet from my thigh, she started to cry. I couldn't say much before I passed out, but I was able to tell her, "Don't worry. It's over."

I didn't realize how full of shit I was until much later. It'd all just begun, and I'd just brought the two of them into hell with me. For the time being though, we were safe. What really matters other than the now?

***

When I woke up, Layla and Darius were on the couch sleeping next to one another. The sun was still out, but it was long enough that the streets seemed to have settled down. I checked my phone. I had a few missed calls. It was mostly some of my old associates asking me if I had anything to do with what they saw on the news. Most of them were snitches; it really didn't require a response.

I wasn't ready to get back to moving yet, but I had a timeline. I had a few things to settle before I left for good.

"Layla." I called to her quietly so that we wouldn't wake Darius. I got up and walked to the bedroom; she followed me with some reluctance.

"I just wanted to explain."

"I don't want to hear it, Tony."

"Listen—"

"No! You promised me that you wouldn't do this shit. I told you everything. I told you I didn't want a part of this life anymore and you brought it to my fucking doorstep!"

"It's not what you think."

"He had a gun to Darius's head, Tony! How delusional do you expect me to be?"

"He had a gun his head, and now he's dead. If you think for one second that I wanted that to happen, you're out of your fucking mind. It wasn't supposed to go down like that. I'm sorry that it did, but he's okay, isn't he?"

"I found him playing with his gun, Tony."

"It was empty."

"That's not the fucking point!"

"Lower your voice. It's done now. Do you understand? It's over. I just have a few more things to take care of, and we can go."

"Go where, Tony?"

"Anywhere. I just need you to trust me."

"I did. I want to. But not after that. I won't let him be like his father. I won't let him be like you. You say you want out, but you don't, Tony. You just want more."

"I want you."

It slipped. I couldn't blame it on the blood loss. I didn't want to. I just wanted her to know. I wanted the two of them to come with me.

"And what about what I want? Did you even think about that?"

"I did. That's why I did what I had to do to make it happen. This shit wasn't easy to get into. It damn sure ain't easy to get out of. But we have a chance to start over. We can be together. Isn't that what you want?"

"Not like this."

"If you know another way, I'm listening."

Darius woke up before she could respond. He must've overheard the yelling. He had something wrapped up in some paper and reached out to give it to me. When I opened it, I saw that it was the chain that the bully had stolen from him a couple days earlier.

"It's broken. Can you fix it?"

"I don't know. I'll try."

He looked at his mother's red and swollen eyes and then back at me.

"Are you leaving again?"

Layla kept her head down and looked away.

"Yeah, I guess so."

"Alright. I'll see you later."

Layla walked me to the front door. I knew I was taking a chance but, when you're swinging for the fences, you don't think much about the collateral damage. My only solution to spontaneity was to double down on it.

"If you change your mind, pack."

I had a cab pick me up a few houses down. I'm not sure why I didn't just call it to the house—I guess I was still a little anxious from earlier. Layla watched from the door until I got in and we pulled off. The driver dropped me off at the safe house where three cars were parked and a few guys were outside waiting for me.

Hopefully, the conversation with Carlos would be more productive.

Out

"You're fucking cuckoo, negro."

"I have my moments."

"When Buzzy called me, I thought that he had finally gone over the deep end. I even brought along a few of my friends—just in case you two would try to pull something."

"I know. I saw them. Did you get the bags?"

"*Si, cabron*. It was quite clever of you to keep them under the tile. Most people don't have the patience for that."

"And our agreement?"

He snapped his fingers, and one of his *associates* dropped a duffel bag of bills in front of me.

"Half a million and some passports, in exchange for everything."

"Good."

"You know, I could've just took the drugs and left you here to hang, hermano. Especially after what happened with my men."

"I thought about that. But you're a businessman like myself. Would it really have been worth the hassle?"

"Don't get cocky, negro. I've *still* got more guns than you."

"So what's your point?"

"I'm a few men down because of your games. I won't hold you responsible. It's on them for not paying attention to orders.

But, there may come a time when I need a favor from you as well."

"A three million dollar profit isn't enough?"

"For the sake of time, let's just say that it's not. When all of this blows over, and you do come back, I may need you for a job. It's hard to find people out here to trust. Most of these clowns out here are looking for the five-year plan. Guys like us, we know the score. We want to see the light at the end of the tunnel."

"And if I say no?"

He laughed at me. I heard some guns cock behind me, as I zipped the bag closed and gripped its handle.

"Say yes, hermano."

"You know how to find me. But since that's the case, I'm gonna need another favor from you as well."

"What's that?"

***

I grabbed the other bag of cash that Lenny had left in the house along with the keys to one of Carlos's extra cars. He didn't give me much grief about it. He seemed confident that we'd be seeing each other again.

I packed up the money and got in the driver's seat. Carlos walked up to the car before I pulled off and offered me some pills for the pain. I turned him down, for obvious reasons. Those fucking things have caused me enough trouble for a lifetime.

"So where will you go now?"

I shrugged and pulled off, then drove to Layla's and waited outside.

It was the first moment in almost a week that I had a second to myself to think about things. I used to take the time to plan my next move, maybe figure out where my next high was coming from or the next job. This time, all I could think about were those few hours that we had—where everything seemed like it would be okay. In those moments, everything was.

It takes a lot of bad moments for you to appreciate the few good ones that you're lucky enough to have. I still didn't want any of my old life. I didn't even want the one that I'd pictured for myself when this all began. The only future I wanted was with her.

I've never been a *praying* man. Technically, most people would tell you that I still ain't. But on that day I was. I put my head on the wheel and thanked whatever it was out there that had kept me alive long enough to get to that moment. That kept me living long enough to feel hope again.

Just before I asked, he delivered. I heard the backdoor of the car spring open. When I popped my head up, I saw Darius with a backpack and some candy, wiggle his way into the seat. Then the passenger side door opened. There she was. She looked nervous, but her movement was definite. She'd later tell me that she was worried about where they would be going, but not about the man that's taking them.

"I'm still pissed at you, Black."

"What happened to Tony?"

"Oh, you gotta earn that one back, honey."

"Looking forward to it."

I put the car in drive and headed for the freeway. I thought it'd be best for us to get out of the city for a little while.

Summer

You have... Eight... New Messages. First Message:
"Yo, yo, yo, Black! It's Buzzy. I just wanted to thank you for hooking me up with lawyer-man. These cops all tryna faze me and shit... But they don't know how *we* get down. I'm about to Johnnie Cochran the shit outta these hoes! I may even snag me one of these sexy-ass CO's. That's right, baby, I see you with yo fine ass! That's right, nigga! They got woman guards up in this bitch. Anyway, how's Central America? You get Ebola yet?—"

Message Erased. Next Message:

"El Negro! I hope that you are enjoying *tu siesta. Mi familia* has told me that you and your girl are doing well. That's good, papa. When you come back I have a job offer for you. As a matter of fact we have much to discuss. It's never too late to pay on a favor, cabron. I hope you're getting rest—"

Message Erased. Next Message:

"Hey man, it's Buzzy. I just wanted to ask: WHO DA' HELL TAKING CARE OF MY MOMMA?! You let me down, Black. Nah, I'm just bullshitting. For real though, is she aight? She ain't been by to come visit me yet this week. And when the hell are you coming back, man? Don't tell me that you went down there and got all assimilated and shit. Aw fuck... *(He begins singing)* Feliz Navidad, *el quiero* taco bell and tater tots... I don't know the fucking lyrics. But don't let Castro twist up yo' mind, man. We need you over here in the states, mainly because my commissary's getting low. There are other reasons, I guess. Peace, negro!"

Message Erased. Next Message:

"Mr Boykins, this is Officer Grant with the New City Police Department. We'd like to ask you some questions about deceased suspect Leonard McDowell and a mutual associate of the two of you... though I suppose just one of you now... A Mr. Christopher Busey. He's also insisted that he goes by the name of Buzzy. We understand that this may be an inconvenience, but as it pertains to the incident on the East Side of town a few weeks ago, any information that you could provide would be very useful. Please give me a call at—"

Message Erased. Next Message:

"Hey man, it's Buzzy again. I just wanted to say—"

Message Erased. Next Message:

"Hello, Tony. It's Buzzy's mom. I just wanted to thank you so much for hiring this home nurse for me. She is just a treat. We watch all my shows. She cooks, she cleans, and I think she's even got a taste for the same kind of reefer. It is just wonderful. It's all so wonderful. God bless you, baby."

Message Erased. Next Message:

"It's Buzzy! Don't delete this serious shit! The three of you have to come home, now! Shit's about to hit the fan in a big bad way. Serious shit, Black. Party's over."

Message Erased. Next Message:

"What's going on Black. It's Vic. I heard about what went down. I'm glad you two took care of that loose end. When you get this bring your ass down to the pen. We've got a lot to discuss. See if you can get Layla to come with you."

This Message Will Be Saved for Twenty-One Days. End of New Messages.

Bullshit never sleeps.

***

Maybe I should've been more attentive to the situation. But I was on vacation. For the foreseeable future all that mattered was that I was free. I had the money. I had the family. We even got a nice little spot for the rest of the summer.

Layla and Darius have been keeping me pretty occupied. We started learning Spanish and got Darius enrolled in some boxing classes. He became a big Manny Pacquiao fan. Layla adjusted pretty well too. She looks even better with a tan.

I'll deal with the bullshit when I get back.

Made in the USA
San Bernardino, CA
21 December 2017